This book is dedicated to my love.
for always being my moon. XC TMLR

"Hello there! Way up high!"

"Were you ever as small as I?"

"My name is Sally. I am a tiny seed."

"I wonder what I will grow to be?"

"Here I am so very small."

"There you are so very tall!"

"I am feeling sad and all alone."

"I am the only seed left. They all have grown."

"Never Fear!"

"Mr. Drop is here!"

"We are friends of four! Let's add Sally to make five!"

"We'll help her grow till she reaches the sky!"

Daisy the sun was so much fun!

Dustin the dirt made sure she didn't get hurt when she fell 3 times that day!

Mr. Drop plopped, plopped, plopped!

"Thanks to Breezy for keeping us cool as we play!"

"Thank you everyone! It's been a great day!"

"Mr. Drop said to Sally "Time for you to sleep! To grow tall, you must go to sleep by Fall!"

Sally closed her eyes and fell asleep in the dirt.

Daisy shined her light on Sally to keep her warm each day.

Sally slept till May!

Mr. Drop woke Sally up with a splash and a smile! "Wake up Sally! You have grown a mile!"

Breezy blew down and swirled around Sally. She gave her a windy tickle!

"We missed you! Wake up! Our sweet little pickle!"

Sally kept growing stronger and taller.

She looked down below at the things that were smaller.

She saw a sad tiny seed.

Sally said "Please don't be sad. Your time to grow is soon!"

"My friends will help you grow as high as the moon!"

"Now, I am so very tall! You are so very small!"

"You will grow as tall as me!"

"I wonder what you will grow to be?"

The End!

CPSIA information can be obtained
at www.ICGtesting.com
Printed in the USA
BVHW011458120821
614274BV00011B/311